MY ADVENTURES

WITH

Disney's

Beauty and the BEAST

This book was especially written for
Gina Colache
With love from
Pop Pop and Mom Mom

© 2002 Disney Enterprises, Inc.
Adapted by Wendy Elks
ISBN 1 875676 17 1

One day, Gina Colache was playing with Allegra, Jessica and Annamarie in the woods near Gina's house at 35 Countrysquire Lane in Marlton. It was the kind of place where magical things happen.

Suddenly, Gina saw a girl in a blue dress coming towards them.

'Would you help me?' asked the girl. 'My name is Belle. I'm looking for my father, Maurice.'

'We haven't seen anyone, but we'll help you look,' said Gina.

'Oh, thank you,' said Belle. 'He went out earlier with our horse, Phillipe, and they haven't come back.'

Just then Phillipe appeared. Maurice wasn't with him.

'Oh, Phillipe, take us to my father!' cried Belle.

Belle, Gina, Allegra, Jessica and Annamarie climbed up into the cart that Phillipe was pulling.

Phillipe took them to a castle deep in the woods. The castle was owned by a selfish prince who, many years ago, had been unkind to an old beggar woman who had come looking for shelter. But the woman was really an enchantress in disguise, and she cast a spell on the castle which turned the uncaring prince into a hideous beast, and his faithful servants into household objects. Ashamed of the way he looked, he hid in his castle surrounded by his enchanted belongings.

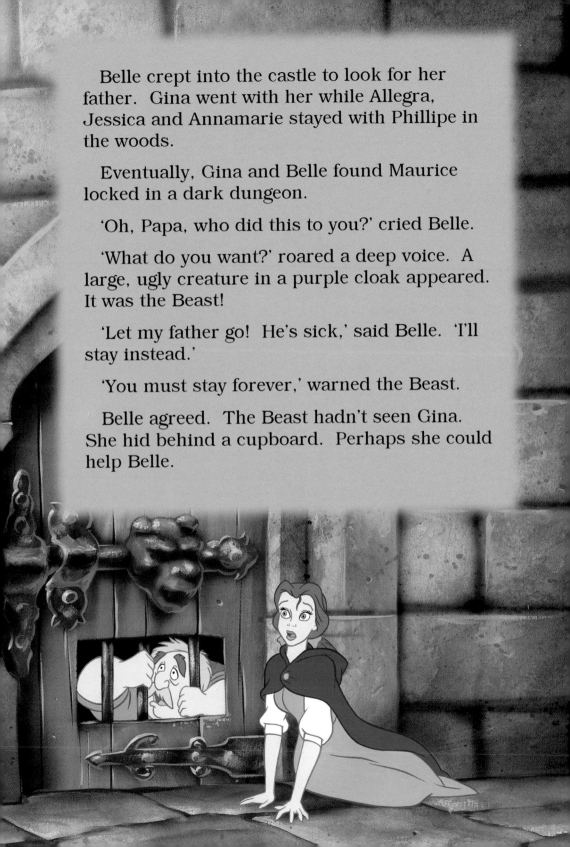

Belle crept into the castle to look for her father. Gina went with her while Allegra, Jessica and Annamarie stayed with Phillipe in the woods.

Eventually, Gina and Belle found Maurice locked in a dark dungeon.

'Oh, Papa, who did this to you?' cried Belle.

'What do you want?' roared a deep voice. A large, ugly creature in a purple cloak appeared. It was the Beast!

'Let my father go! He's sick,' said Belle. 'I'll stay instead.'

'You must stay forever,' warned the Beast.

Belle agreed. The Beast hadn't seen Gina. She hid behind a cupboard. Perhaps she could help Belle.

The Beast dragged Maurice out of the castle and let him go, leaving Belle in his place.

'Don't worry, Belle,' said Gina. 'I'll go for help.'

'No, please stay with me!' cried Belle. 'But don't let the Beast see you.'

Gina followed as the Beast took Belle to her room.

'You can go anywhere in the castle, except the West Wing. That is FORBIDDEN!' ordered the Beast before he left.

Gina crept into Belle's room followed by the Beast's enchanted servants — a talking clock called Cogsworth, Mrs. Potts, the teapot, and her son Chip.

'Welcome,' said Cogsworth, bowing.

Later, after a wonderful dinner with entertainment from the enchanted creatures, Gina and Belle explored the castle. They crept into the West Wing, even though the Beast had told them not to go there.

They discovered a strange, glowing rose covered by a glass case.

'Oh, look!' cried Belle. She was just about to touch it when the Beast came in. Gina quickly hid behind a curtain.

'Don't touch that rose!' bellowed the Beast.

Belle and Gina didn't know it, but the rose was magical. It would bloom until the Beast's twenty-first birthday. If he could learn to love and be loved in return before that day, then the spell would be broken. If not, he would remain a beast forever.

The Beast growled so much at Belle for disobeying him that she fled from the castle. Now Gina was alone — and afraid.

Gina went back to Belle's room and Mrs. Potts and Chip kept her company for a while. Soon, Belle returned!

'I ran away, but wolves surrounded me in the forest,' Belle told them. 'The Beast saved me, but he was hurt by the wolves. I'm going to look after him.'

'Did you see Allegra, Jessica and Annamarie outside the castle?' asked Gina.

'They had to go home,' said Belle. 'Where do you live, Gina?'

'At 35 Countrysquire Lane in Marlton,' said Gina.

'I hope you can stay a bit longer, and keep me company,' said Belle.

'I will,' promised Gina.

Belle and the Beast soon became friends. Gina watched from an upstairs window while he and Belle walked in the garden.

Later, the Beast showed Belle his library. 'You can have all of this,' he told her. 'I want you to be happy.'

'I miss my father,' said Belle. 'Can I go to him? That would make me very happy.'

The Beast shook his head sadly. He liked having Belle with him.

That night Belle went downstairs to have dinner with the Beast. She was wearing a new dress, and she looked beautiful. The Beast had made a special effort to look nice, too.

They toasted their newfound friendship. After the meal, Belle persuaded the Beast to dance with her in the magnificent ballroom. The Beast looked down at her. Strange feelings inside him were growing stronger.

Gina watched the happy dancing couple with Lumiere the candlestick and Cogsworth.

'Could this be true love?' wondered Lumiere. 'If so, the spell will be broken.'

'What spell?' asked Gina.

Cogsworth explained about the magical rose.

'I think the Beast might be falling in love,' smiled Gina.

'They must both fall in love to break the spell,' reminded Cogsworth.

'Are you happy here?' the Beast asked
Belle later that night.

Belle sighed. 'I would like to see my
father.'

'Here, look into my enchanted mirror,' said
the Beast. Belle saw her father. He looked
very sick!

'Oh no! I must go to him!' cried Belle.

'Very well,' said the Beast. 'I will let you
go, but take the mirror to remember me by.'

He watched sadly as Belle ran from the castle and whistled for Phillipe.

'You shouldn't have let her go. She's our last hope!' Lumiere cried.

'I had to. I love her,' said the Beast sadly.

Gina ran from the castle, too. Belle waited for her, and pulled her up onto Phillipe's broad back. Gina hung on tightly as they galloped back to town.

When they arrived, they saw Maurice being led away by Gaston, a horrible bully who wanted to marry Belle.

'Maurice is crazy,' said Gaston. 'He said you were being kept prisoner by a monster.'

'My father isn't crazy! And the Beast isn't a monster! You are!' cried Belle.

'You like this hideous creature?' he asked Belle, as he showed the villagers the Beast's reflection in the enchanted mirror.

'He's a monster! We must KILL him!' he cried.

Gaston locked Maurice and Belle inside their house and led the villagers off to find the Beast.

As soon as they were gone, Gina rushed to unlock the door.

'Oh, thank you, Gina!' cried Belle. 'Will you go back to the castle with me? We must try to save the Beast!'

'Yes, I'll come,' said Gina.

Once again Belle and Gina climbed onto Phillipe. As they rode back through the forest, large drops of rain began to fall. A storm was coming!

Meanwhile, Gaston and the villagers were pounding the door of the castle with a huge tree trunk. Inside, Mrs. Potts pleaded with the heartbroken Beast to defend himself.

'Remember, the Beast is mine!' shouted Gaston.

Gina held on tightly to Belle's waist as Phillipe galloped along the winding trail towards the castle. She wished Allegra, Jessica and Annamarie were there to help defend the Beast from Gaston and the villagers!

In the distance they heard a pounding noise, followed by shouting and cheering. The villagers had broken into the castle!

When the villagers entered the castle, everything was silent. Then, as if from nowhere, Cogsworth yelled, 'NOW!'

Suddenly, all the furniture and pots and pans came to life! The villagers were attacked by cupboards, plates, spoons, and forks. It was a magnificent battle. While it was raging, Gaston disappeared quietly. He was looking for the Beast.

Belle and Gina slid off the panting horse. Where was the Beast? Suddenly they saw him and Gaston on the balcony above them. Gaston shot him with an arrow, and laughed when he howled with pain.

'NO!' cried Belle. 'Don't hurt him!'

'Do you love her, Beast? Do you think she could love you when she can have me?' laughed Gaston.

The Beast roared at Gaston and leapt down to the terrace where Gina and Belle stood.

'Look out!' yelled Gina. Gaston had followed the Beast. He plunged his knife into the Beast's back. But then Gaston slipped and fell into the dark, flowing water below them.

'Gaston's gone forever,' Gina told them, looking over the side of the terrace.

The wounded Beast fell into Belle's arms.

'You came back,' he whispered. Then he slipped to the ground, and lay still.

'Yes. I love you,' Belle told him.

At that moment, up in the West Wing of the castle, the last petal was falling from the enchanted rose.

Belle sobbed as she held the Beast tightly. Suddenly a bright, swirling light began to shine down on the Beast and his body rose up into the air, and slowly transformed into...

...a handsome prince!

Gina gasped. She'd never seen such magic! As Belle and the Prince kissed for the first time, the magic light transformed the entire castle.

Gina watched in amazement as Cogsworth turned into a butler, and Mrs. Potts became the housekeeper.

'Oh, Gina! I hope you're going to stay with us,' said Mrs. Potts.

'Yes, stay!' begged Lumiere. 'There's going to be a wedding! The spell is broken! I told you Belle was the one!'

'Excuse me, I told you,' said Cogsworth.

The prince and Belle didn't hear Cogsworth and Lumiere arguing. They only had eyes for each other.

'I can't stay,' said Gina. 'I must go home to Marlton. But I could come and visit and I could bring Allegra, Jessica and Annamarie, too.'

'You will always be welcome here,' the prince told her. 'You have been a good friend to Belle. Take this sweet pea and keep it in a special place to remember us by.'

'The sweet pea is my birth flower. My birthday is on April 20th!' exclaimed Gina.

'You will always be my friend, Gina,' said Belle. 'And you must come back for our wedding which, in your honor, will be held on April 20th.'

And do you know what? She did.

This personalized Disney's Beauty and the Beast book was specially created for Gina Colache of 35 Countrysquire Lane, Marlton NJ with love from Pop Pop and Mom Mom.

Additional books ordered may be mailed separately - please allow a few days for differences in delivery times.

If you would like to receive additional My Adventure Book order forms, please contact:

My Adventure Books
PO Box 9203
Central Islip NY 11722-9203

Phone: (952) 703 5529
www.identitydirect.com